A E

written by Pam Holden
illustrated by Kelvin Hawley

B is for bat.

C is for cave.

C is for crab.

B is for beach.

B is for bee.

F is for flowers.

S is for snake.

G is for grass.

C is for crocodile.

R is for river.

S is for spider.

W is for web.

W is for whale.

S is for sea.

M is for mouse.